DATE DUE

Serious Science

Also by Janice Lee Smith

The Monster in the Third Dresser Drawer
And Other Stories About Adam Joshua

The Kid Next Door and Other Headaches
More Stories About Adam Joshua

The Show-and-Tell War
And Other Stories About Adam Joshua

It's Not Easy Being George
Stories About Adam Joshua (And His Dog)

The Turkeys' Side of It
Adam Joshua's Thanksgiving

There's a Ghost in the Coatroom
Adam Joshua's Christmas

Nelson in Love
An Adam Joshua Valentine's Day Story

Serious Science

An Adam Joshua Story
BY JANICE LEE SMITH

drawings by Dick Gackenbach

HarperCollins*Publishers*

SERIOUS SCIENCE
An Adam Joshua Story
Text copyright © 1993 by Janice Lee Smith
Illustrations copyright © 1993 by Dick Gackenbach
Printed in the United States
of America. For information address HarperCollins
Children's Books, a division of HarperCollins Publishers,
10 East 53rd Street, New York, NY 10022.
           1   2   3   4   5   6   7   8   9   10
                              ❖
                        First Edition

Library of Congress Cataloging-in-Publication Data
Smith, Janice Lee, date
   Serious science : an Adam Joshua story / by Janice Lee
Smith ; drawings by Dick Gackenbach.
       p.   cm.
   Summary: Devastated when his little sister and his dog
George demolish his science project on the solar system,
Adam Joshua becomes ingenious and inventive in coming
up with a last-minute replacement.
   ISBN 0-06-020779-5. — ISBN 0-06-020782-5 (lib. bdg.)
   [1. Science projects—Fiction.   2. Schools—Fiction.]
I. Gackenbach, Dick, ill.   II. Title.
PZ7.S6499Se   1993   91-30824
[Fic]—dc20   CIP
                                                AC

To My Brave Nephews:
Dain,
Randy,
Marc,
and Adam.
And to Jessica, My Dauntless Niece.

Chapter One

Down at the other end of the school where the older kids had classes, a really terrific Science Fair was being planned.

All morning long the sounds of excitement had been drifting up the hall.

All morning long Adam Joshua's class had been listening to it, and Adam Joshua wasn't the only one feeling insulted about being left out.

"I mean, I don't get it," Angie said with a scowl. "It's not like they're smarter or more scientific or anything just because they're older. I've known my big sister for a long time, and she's as dumb now as she ever was."

Everybody who had a dumb big brother or sister nodded. Adam Joshua only had a little sister, but he nodded along. Amanda Jane was smart for a baby, but she'd probably get dumber as she got older.

"I'm the scientific one in my family," said Angie. "Not my sister. Some of my ideas will probably save the world someday, so I'm the one who should get a chance to get started."

Actually, Adam Joshua had been planning to save the world himself, but it was fine with him if Angie wanted to help.

"Well, my big brother's dumb AND disgusting," Sidney grumbled. "He decided to do his science experiment to see if our cat, Fleabitten, really has nine lives."

Everybody looked disgusted along with Sidney. Adam Joshua was just glad his dog, George, wasn't here to hear this.

"He was going to put the cat in the dryer for the first life," said Sidney, "and I didn't think Fleabitten could last through the rest of the experiments my brother was planning. I had

2

to tell my parents, and they made him stop."

"If the world's counting on my sister to save it, it's going to be in for a big shock," muttered Angie. She stopped talking and thought a minute. "What's your brother going to do now?" she asked Sidney, worried.

"Now he wants to do the same experiments and use me," Sidney said, looking depressed.

———

Everybody had been on their best behavior lately because their teacher, Ms. D., was going to have a baby and they wanted to be considerate. On the other hand, since they'd been on their best behavior, they thought they could probably get away with a little pouting now.

So everyone switched from looking grumpy and tried looking tragic and pathetic instead. When it came to Ms. D., that usually worked best. Several people threw in a little cute for good measure.

Ms. D. tried ignoring them for a while, but the cute was hard to resist.

"Okay, I give up," she finally said, laughing. "I'll go tell the big guys that they'll have to

3

move over at the Science Fair because we're bringing our experiments and inventions too."

Everybody cheered and looked smug and satisfied.

"I'll try to be there for it," Sidney told Ms. D. "I'm just hoping that after the dryer and everything else, I'll still be around."

———

Now that they'd won, everybody started making great plans, and they made sure they were nice and noisy about it so the older kids could hear.

"I just love science," Heidi said. "My big sister did this really great science experiment where she grew a whole bunch of the same plants, but she played different music for them and they grew at different rates. We still have the plants, so I'll start playing music for them again. It'll be really neat."

It sounded really neat. Everybody was really sorry they hadn't thought of it first.

"My father's a doctor," Philip said happily. "And he cuts people open all the time. Maybe he's got somebody left over I could cut open too."

Everybody looked like they were going to be sick, and they all moved far away from Philip.

"A lot of scientists have animals run in mazes," Angie told them. "So I'm going to have my hamster, Walton Nine, run in a maze to get his food. I'll time him and keep charts and stuff to show he's getting faster."

Nobody had any idea what hamsters had to do with Angie saving the world, but they all got worried. Her hamsters were always nearly dying or totally dead. Nobody was sure an Angie hamster could make it through a maze even once.

"I can add ramps and maybe a wheel," said Angie, "and all sorts of things to make it more fun for Walton." She got out paper and cheerfully started to draw up plans.

Adam Joshua got out paper and sketched a little himself. He was the best in the class when it came to knowing about planets and stars and moon stuff. What he wanted to do was put together the solar system, maybe out of Styrofoam balls or something. Then everybody who wanted to help save the world could see what it was they were trying to save.

Everybody gathered close to look at Adam Joshua's sketch.

Elliot Banks crowded in most.

Several people ohhhed. Several people ahhhed. Elliot Banks snickered.

"You're so smart, Adam Joshua," Heidi said. "I wish I knew all that stuff."

A lot of people nodded. Elliot Banks stopped snickering and crowded in closer to get a better look.

Adam Joshua tried to look modest.

"That's going to be a great project," Angie said. "I'll bet it's even the best one."

Modest wasn't working out too well. Adam Joshua settled for trying not to look too pleased with himself.

Elliot Banks walked away looking very thoughtful.

———

"I already know what I'm going to do," Adam Joshua's best friend, Nelson, told him on their walk home after school. "I'm going to prove my fish have ESP. They always seem to know what I'm thinking, so I hardly ever have to say anything to them out loud. And I'm

pretty sure my boss fish, Julius, has been thinking me the answers to my math problems when I do homework each night."

Nelson stayed happy until he got ready to turn off to his house.

Then he turned a little gloomy.

"Of course," Nelson said, sighing, "I'm going to have to do all my experimenting with Henry around. I'll bet real scientists hardly ever have to put up with two-year-olds."

Adam Joshua faced his front door with gloom too. His little sister, Amanda Jane, was the same age as Henry, and most days it was hard to tell which one of them was worse.

He went inside quietly. Amanda Jane left trails wherever she went, and there were a lot of trails around, but Amanda Jane didn't seem to be at this end of any of them. Adam Joshua's dog, George, usually met him after school each afternoon, but he didn't seem to be around either.

Adam Joshua tiptoed up the stairs, picking his way through a trail made up of an unrolled roll of toilet tissue, a teakettle, a stuffed dog that looked a lot like George after a bad day, some of Adam Joshua's underwear, and bits and pieces of Amanda Jane's lunch.

He'd never figured he'd see the day when his room would be the cleanest place in the house.

The great thing about the solar system was that everything was round. Adam Joshua was terrible at art, but fine with circles.

He got out paper and markers, drew a big circle for the sun, made planets in several sizes of medium, and added little circles for moons and Pluto.

He'd just meant to do a blueprint, but it was turning out so terrific, he decided he'd put it in his exhibit. It was absolutely the best drawing he'd ever made.

"Absolutely," he said. George would love it.

Adam Joshua thought that if Nelson's fish had ESP, George probably did too.

"Here, George," he thought hard, concentrating.

George didn't show up. On the other hand, George only came when he wanted to even if you called out loud.

Adam Joshua went into the hall and followed Amanda Jane's trail until it led to his parents' bedroom closet.

He found George inside, buried under a pile of stuff with Amanda Jane.

George looked delighted to be rescued. As soon as Adam Joshua unwrapped him from ties, took a hanger off his ear, and unhooked a purse from around his neck, he streaked out of the closet.

"AdamGeorgeshishbangzinger!" Amanda Jane screeched, throwing shoes after them.

George definitely looked like he'd heard Adam Joshua's ESP, and like he would have come on the double if the closet doorknob had been easier to manage.

George also threw a little disgusted into the look, because he'd been thinking "Help!" for quite a while himself, and he thought Adam Joshua could have gotten to the rescuing part a little sooner.

"Sorry," Adam Joshua ESP'd with a chuckle, hugging George close.

Chapter Two

"My ESP experiment's going great, Adam Joshua," Nelson said the next morning on their way to school. "First I made a lot of cards and put different numbers on them. I just hold the cards up so I can see the numbers but my fish can't. Then they tell me what they think's on the card by the number of times they swish their tails."

Adam Joshua thought he might try it with George sometime, although he wasn't too sure George knew his numbers to begin with.

"And I went ahead and asked Julius for all

the answers to my math homework too," Nelson said happily. "It really saved a lot of time."

Adam Joshua decided he'd get to work teaching George his numbers as soon as possible.

———

Quite a few people were already in the classroom when Adam Joshua and Nelson walked in, and all of them were talking about their science projects.

Sidney was still around and trying to stay out of his big brother's way. "I thought of a great experiment," he told them proudly. "I went into my brother's bedroom while he was out, and I collected all his dirty socks. They were really disgusting," Sidney said, sounding delighted. "Some were in a pizza box with old pizza, and a bunch were lying in puddles of milk or grape juice, and some were lying in some stuff I didn't look at too closely because I didn't want to know what it was."

"Yecch!" everybody said. Several turned a little green.

"Yeah, it was great!" said Sidney. "I sprinkled a little water on the socks and put them in plastic bags back in the corner of my closet. I figure they'll grow all kinds of things."

The people who'd been looking a little green looked a little greener.

"My brother would have clobbered me if he'd caught me," Sidney said, looking serious.

Everybody nodded solemnly. They'd all met Sidney's brother, and hearing that he was going to put the cat in the dryer had come as no surprise.

"So it was dangerous," Sidney said with a shiver, "but definitely worth it."

———

Ralph came bustling into the classroom and headed straight for the science table in the corner.

"I'm going to do a study of fingerprints," he told everybody, setting out paper and ink pads. "Fingerprint studies are very scientific, and I want to be a private eye when I grow up, so it's a good chance to get started."

If Adam Joshua could have done two projects, fingerprints definitely would have been the second one.

Ralph put up a sign.

VOLUNTEERS
TO BE
FINGER PRINTED

P.S. FOR PEOPLE WHO MIGHT BE IN TROUBLE WITH THE POLICE SHOULD'NT VOLUNTEER

"VOLUNTEERS," it read, "TO BE FINGER-PRINTED."

Adam Joshua hurried over to the science table so he'd be first, and everybody lined up behind him, and they all started rolling up their sleeves.

Ralph looked at his sign thoughtfully for a minute, and then he added a note.

"P.S.," he wrote, "PEOPLE WHO MIGHT BE IN TROUBLE WITH THE POLICE SHOULDN'T VOLUNTEER."

"Private eyes have to turn any bad guys they find over to the police," Ralph explained. "And I'd feel really awful if I had to turn some-body over who was just trying to help me out."

Everybody stopped in the middle of the sleeve rolling and stood there thinking a minute. Adam Joshua was pretty sure he didn't have anything to worry about, and most of the other people decided to take their chances and be fingerprinted too.

But several people turned pale, pulled their sleeves down tight, and hurried off, watching Ralph nervously over their shoulders.

Adam Joshua gave Ralph some incredibly great fingerprints, and then he went down the hall to wash his hands.

When he got back to the classroom, Sidney was giving Ralph a nose print too.

"You never can tell what you might need," said Sidney.

Ms. D. came in the door right behind Adam Joshua.

"And I thought Mr. D. was right behind me," she told him, turning around with a puzzled look. "He's bringing us a skeleton for the classroom."

Evidently the skeleton didn't want to come.

They heard an awful lot of bone rattling and crashing, and it sounded like Mr. D. was at the losing end of most of it.

"Uh-oh," said Sidney. "It got him."

Mr. D. and the skeleton both fell in the door at the same time, and there were so many arms and legs everywhere, it was a little hard to tell who had won.

Everybody hurried over. Adam Joshua

sorted out the skeleton's feet first, and then Mr. D.'s, and helped get them both standing again.

"A friend of a friend," Mr. D. said, trying to catch his breath. "We thought you might like to borrow him for inspiration since you're being scientific."

Nobody was about to say they didn't feel any too inspired by skeletons.

"Mortimer Flugg," Mr. D. panted, setting the skeleton up in the corner. "He was a lion tamer, but he wasn't very good at it."

Everybody looked the skeleton over closely.

Everybody noticed rows of little nicks, and a lot of eyes got a whole lot wider.

"Yep," Mr. D. said, sighing sadly, "teeth marks."

———

Mr. D. left after a final glare at Mortimer, and Ms. D. walked him down the hall.

"My dad said he was sorry, but he was all out of people I could operate on," Philip told everyone glumly. "He promised to put one of my signs up in his office though."

Philip started to tape a sign up on the coatroom door too, but since everyone was over by Mortimer Flugg, he went over and taped his sign on the skeleton's hands instead.

"VOLUNTEERS NEEDED," it read, "FOR FREE OPERATIONS."

"You can choose what part you'd like operated on," Philip called after everyone as they scurried away. "I've been studying the pictures in my dad's books on all of them."

Philip and the skeleton were left standing in the corner all alone.

"I think my father operated on you," Philip told Mort.

———

Adam Joshua settled in his chair, took the finished drawing of the solar system out of his backpack, and laid it on the desk just in case anybody going by wanted to look at it.

He wasn't a bit surprised when a lot of people did.

"It's just incredible, Adam Joshua," Angie said. "I never knew Saturn was so beautiful."

"And I never knew Pluto was so tiny," said Heidi.

Everyone started passing the drawing

around, which didn't bother Adam Joshua too much until he lost sight of it.

"That's because Elliot grabbed it away from Sidney," Angie told him. "He's over in the corner now, taking all sorts of notes about it."

Going anywhere near Elliot Banks was something Adam Joshua absolutely and totally tried to avoid, but there wasn't much else to do.

He gritted his teeth into a smile and went over to stand beside Elliot.

"Excuse me," he said, trying to sound polite through clenched teeth, "I need to get that back now. Ms. D. was wanting to see it."

Actually, Ms. D. didn't know she was wanting to see it, but Adam Joshua was sure she did.

"I don't know why," Elliot said, taking his time and taking a few more notes. "It's really stupid."

Elliot held the drawing up for Adam Joshua to take, except that when Adam Joshua did, Elliot smirked and yanked it back again so that the paper ripped right down the middle.

"Whoops," said Elliot, smirking more. "Stupid and torn."

———

By the time Adam Joshua had finished taping the solar system back together again, the world looked a little bent out of shape. And since a lot of people had forgotten to wash their hands after volunteering for Ralph, Adam Joshua ended up with blue ink fingerprints on most of the major planets.

"It's turning out to be a lousy morning, George," Adam Joshua ESP'd home before he settled down to work.

———

Nelson spent a lot of the day trying to convince Ms. D. that Julius was the one who'd gotten all the answers wrong on his math homework.

"But I don't think she ever believed me," Nelson said glumly after school. "She even gave me extra work sheets for tonight, so I can get some extra practice."

Adam Joshua decided to wait on teaching George numbers until he could teach him adding and subtracting too. It was just as well, because he couldn't wait to get started on his solar system, and he figured it was going to take every minute he had.

"I don't know how I'm going to tell Julius," Nelson said.

———

One of the worst things about Amanda Jane was that she always seemed to know what was going on, especially if it was something that you didn't want her anywhere near.

She was lying in wait outside Adam Joshua's bedroom when he got there, and when he tried to sneak in his door, she zoomed right by him and settled in the middle of his paints and all the Styrofoam balls for his planets with a squeal of delight.

For a little kid, Amanda Jane always put up a good fight. By the time Adam Joshua hauled her out of his room, she'd pulled his hair, clobbered him on the nose, bitten him on the leg, and shrieked a fair number of amazingly rotten things.

George showed up to help, but it was never quite clear whose side he was on.

"But thank you anyway," Adam Joshua said, scooting him out the door right behind Amanda Jane. "And I'm sorry about this part, but you like to chew on things."

George wasn't about to apologize. It was true. He did.

Adam Joshua locked his door and checked it twice before he got to work.

Considering the babies and dogs he had around, he wasn't about to take any chances.

Chapter Three

Getting ready for the Science Fair was a lot more work than anyone had counted on. On the other hand, Adam Joshua thought that if a person wanted to save the world someday, he'd probably have to make a few sacrifices.

Every day Sidney's brother came to school without any socks on, and every day he seemed to look a little more suspicious and madder about it.

"But the socks are growing really great stuff," Sidney told them excitedly. "One's growing a green furry mold, and one's growing an orange bumpy fungus stuff, and one's even growing these little tiny mushrooms."

Adam Joshua got a little alarmed. He always threw his dirty socks on the bedroom floor, and George always chewed on them.

Still, Amanda Jane chewed on them too, and they didn't seem to slow her down any.

"And I think one sock is growing something purple that's never been grown before," Sidney said, very proud.

———

Ralph brought in *The Big Book of Crooks and Their Fingerprints*.

"It's great!" he said, showing everybody pictures of some nasty-looking bad guys. "Now I can see if any of the fingerprints I've taken match any of these."

The people who hadn't been worried before they let Ralph fingerprint them started worrying now.

———

Some experiments weren't going too well.

"My tape recorder broke," Heidi told Adam Joshua. "So I decided to *sing* different music to all my plants. But now none of them are looking that great."

"Walton Nine isn't looking that great either," Angie said, looking discouraged too. "All this maze stuff is making him really nervous."

Philip gave up trying to get people to let him operate on them.

"Never mind," he told them, disgusted. "My dad's got a lot of people parts in jars at the hospital. I'll borrow some and just make my exhibit out of those."

Nobody had the nerve to ask where the parts had come from.

Philip started making a list.

"Heart," he said, thinking out loud. "Brain, an eyeball or two, maybe a lung, a liver, a . . ."

Luckily, in the stampede to get away from Philip, everybody held on to their own parts just fine.

———

Mr. D. came by to make sure the skeleton was staying where he'd put him.

"He's quiet, but he's tricky," Mr. D. said, watching Mortimer suspiciously.

"I just wish he'd stop smiling," Angie

complained. "It's really hard to do work sheets with a skeleton grinning at you all the time."

"He tries to make the best of things," Mr. D. said, wiping a tear from his eye.

Ralph fingerprinted Mr. D.

Then he remembered to show Mr. D. the sign and warn him about the police.

"Oh, no! Now you tell me," Mr. D. groaned, smacking himself on the forehead and leaving it fingerprinted too.

"Well, there's nothing to do about it now," Mr. D. said. "I guess when you match them up, you'll have to haul me in."

He snarled and tried to look tough and crookish, and he limped his way along.

Ms. D. was just coming through the door. The more pregnant she'd gotten, the longer the coming through took. Mr. D. stood back chuckling until she made it, and then he gave her a gangsterish tweak on the nose as he passed on by.

Ralph got busy with his book of crooks' fingerprints right away.

"I'm pretty sure your husband's a bad guy in disguise," he told Ms. D. "I just can't figure out which one yet."

"I'm sorry to hear it," Ms. D. said.

"He's maybe Clumsy Clyde or Haphazard Harry."

"That would explain a lot of things," Ms. D. muttered as she worked on getting Mr. D.'s fingerprints off her nose.

———

"Remember, it's just two days till the Science Fair," Ms. D. reminded them one afternoon as they headed out the door after school.

"I guess I'd better get started," several people said.

"I'm nearly finished with my project, Adam Joshua," Nelson told him on their walk home. "My fish did great on their ESP tests, so I've made charts showing how many times they got the numbers right with their tails. Now my fish Julius is telling me all about his dreams, and I'm going to do some drawings of them for my exhibit too."

Adam Joshua listened to Nelson with half an ear, which was actually half an ear more than he usually used when Nelson was talking about his fish.

The other ear and a half and all the rest of him was busy working out the plans for finishing up his own project.

He felt like he'd been painting planets forever, but now he was down to just the final details, and everything looked fantastic.

Tonight his parents were going to help him hang all the planets and moons from coat hangers. And he had it figured that if he turned all the hangers just right, and kept the strings straight, everything would revolve perfectly.

"Fish dreams," Nelson told him, "can really be strange."

———

When Adam Joshua got home, Amanda Jane and George were in the kitchen. George was being buried under a mountain of pots and pans, but he looked resigned to it.

Adam Joshua hurried up the stairs to his room, locked the door, and settled down to work.

The green on the earth was dry, so he painted in the final blue for the oceans.

He looked at the earth for a minute, and

then he painted a tiny red "X" where his house would be, and added a drawing of himself waving out at everybody in space. He drew George beside him smiling.

Adam Joshua had been proud of a lot of things in his life, but this solar system was going to be right up there. And Ms. D. didn't know it yet, but he planned to give it to her for the classroom.

Some things you just had to share.

———

Adam Joshua worked along, and through the window he could see Nelson over in his room doing the same.

When Nelson got up and left after a while, Adam Joshua didn't think a lot about it. He figured listening to a fish tell you his dreams could wear anybody out.

And when he noticed that Nelson had left his door standing open, it worried him a little, but he was more worried about getting the big red spot on Jupiter exactly right, and painting took all his concentration.

So it came as a big shock when he looked up again and saw Henry reaching into the aquar-

ium with a happy, hungry look in his eye.

Nelson was getting a drink of water when Adam Joshua burst through his back door yelling, but he started yelling right along, and charged with Adam Joshua through the house and up the stairs without asking a thing about it.

They skidded into Nelson's bedroom, and once Nelson saw what he was yelling about, he started yelling a whole lot louder.

Adam Joshua tackled Henry just as Henry was putting Julius into his mouth headfirst.

Julius soared out of Henry's hand and did a great flying fish imitation, and Nelson made an incredible leap and caught him.

Nelson kept right on yelling while he tucked Julius back into the aquarium and scooted Henry out into the hall. He scooted Adam Joshua out right after, then slammed and locked the door.

"You're welcome," Adam Joshua called back.

Henry didn't look any too grateful either.

——————

When Adam Joshua got home again, it was

very quiet. The pots and pans Amanda Jane and George had been playing with were scattered across the living room and led in a trail up the stairs.

Adam Joshua started yelling before he made it to the top.

He'd left in such a panic, he'd left his own bedroom door standing wide open. Now the sounds of baby giggling and dog munching drifted out of it.

Amanda Jane was sitting in the middle of all the planets, chomping away on what was left of Jupiter.

George was snacking on Pluto, and there were pieces of Mars, Earth, and all the rest of the planets and moons scattered everywhere.

"Shadawahdiscookie," Amanda Jane told him cheerfully as she spit out Jupiter and took another bite of Neptune.

―――――

While his mother took Amanda Jane to the doctor, Adam Joshua tried to put his world back together again.

"My mother said Amanda Jane isn't going to

die or anything," he told George. "But the doctor wanted to make sure she didn't get sick.

"The vet said you might get a little sick, but probably not. I wouldn't mind," he said sadly, "if you both got very sick."

George had the decency to look a little ashamed, but not the least bit sick.

Besides half of Jupiter, there was really nothing left.

Adam Joshua felt sick enough for everybody.

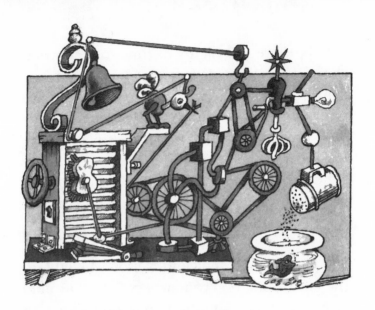

Chapter Four

"That's terrible, Adam Joshua," Nelson said horrified the next morning on their way to school. "If you want to remake all your planets and stuff, I'll help you remake them."

Adam Joshua sighed a deep and tragic sigh.

"My parents said they'd help too," he said, shaking his head. "But the Science Fair's tomorrow, and there just isn't enough time to get it all done."

Still, there was plenty of time to feel rotten about it, which made it worse.

And normally Adam Joshua would have talked to George about his problems, but he didn't feel much like it this time, since George had helped create most of them.

Besides, since George had ESP, he'd probably heard everything Adam Joshua was thinking about him anyway.

———

When Adam Joshua and Nelson walked into the classroom, everyone was gathered around Mortimer Flugg singing him a song about leg bones being connected to hip bones.

Mortimer looked like he was trying to grin and bear it.

Philip was grumbling because he hadn't been able to borrow the jars of people parts after all.

"My dad said somebody might need them for something," Philip told them. "And he said I'd feel bad if somebody couldn't find a brain because I had it. It seemed to me I need it as much as anybody else," Philip groused. "So I didn't think I'd feel all that bad."

Ms. D. came in the door, and Mr. D. staggered in behind her carrying something big and weird.

"Also ugly," Sidney told him.

"It's a masterpiece," Mr. D. said proudly, setting it down.

"It's still ugly," Sidney said, and everybody else gathered around and nodded in agreement.

Whatever it was, it had a lot of levers, pulleys, and wheels. It also had an eggbeater, a washboard, and a bell.

"The Frankly Fantastic Fully Foolproof Fine Fish Food Fancy Fish Feeder," Mr. D. told them modestly. "I thought you might find it inspiring."

Nobody looked any too inspired.

"It's to feed my goldfish, Cuddles," Mr. D. said.

Nelson got very interested and moved in to get a better look.

Mr. D. flipped a switch and everything geared up with a lot of clanking. It was fairly amazing for a few minutes. Wheels turned, pulleys pulled, levers lifted, and the eggbeater whirled, although Adam Joshua never saw the washboard do much of anything at all.

Finally, the bell rang to tell Cuddles breakfast was served, and the box tipped so that fish food sprinkled down into the fish bowl.

Cuddles zoomed up to do his part for science and eat.

Nelson turned a little pale and moved back beside Adam Joshua.

"I don't think he understands a thing about having fish," Nelson said. "If he feeds them that way, he doesn't even get to pet them."

"I plan to make one for the baby too," Mr. D. said, satisfied.

———

Between the fish feeder and Mortimer it was a little hard to get anybody's attention, but Adam Joshua worked at it because he figured he could use all the sympathy he could get.

Except that just as he started to tell everybody about The Great Amanda Jane Disaster, Elliot Banks walked in the door carrying an

40

absolutely enormous, incredibly beautiful model of the solar system.

People went crazy. Some shrieked, and some gasped, and quite a few shouted things like "Wow!" and "Good grief!" and "Look at that!"

Sidney yelled, "Zounds!" because he'd learned it recently and had been waiting for a good chance to work it in.

"You didn't yell, 'Zounds!' for my fish feeder," Mr. D. told him, sounding hurt.

Everybody but Adam Joshua gathered around while Elliot placed the model carefully on the science table.

Adam Joshua placed his forehead carefully down on his desk and kept it there so he wouldn't bang it.

"And you'll never believe this," Elliot said smugly, keeping his eye on Adam Joshua as he flipped a switch on the model.

The world revved up, and small moons started revolving around their planets, and all the planets started making their way around the sun.

People went even crazier. A lot of them

yelled, "Zounds!" now that they knew it, and Mr. D. glared at all of them.

Adam Joshua buried his head deeper into his desktop, which wasn't easy considering it was wood.

"I plan to give it to you for the class," Elliot told Ms. D. at his most smug. "It's the best money could buy."

"Well, that's wonderful, Elliot," Ms. D. said. "Why don't you give us a talk now along with the demonstration and let us know a little bit about each planet."

Elliot looked fairly dumbfounded, and really mad.

"You can't expect me to know all that stuff," he told Ms. D.

"You'd be surprised how much I expect," Ms. D. told him firmly with a no-nonsense look in her eye.

———

Mr. D. kept demonstrating his fish feeder for everybody. Cuddles was a good sport, and he managed to keep up with the eating until he looked positively green around the gills.

Finally, Nelson hurried over.

"Your fish ESP'd me a message," he told Mr. D.

"Fantastic," Mr. D. said, beaming at Cuddles. "What?"

"He said, 'Enough's enough!'" Nelson scolded sternly, taking the box of fish food away.

Sidney volunteered to fill in for Cuddles.

"Except I'd prefer chocolate-covered raisins," he said.

"I only brought fish food," Mr. D. said sadly as he packed up the fish feeder to head home.

Sidney thought about it a minute.

"What flavor?" he finally asked.

———

After Elliot, Adam Joshua wasn't much in the mood to tell anybody about the end of his world. He plodded through the morning's work, and waited until everybody else had gone out for recess before he went up to tell Ms. D.

"That's the most rotten thing I've ever heard," she said, giving him a hug.

Actually, Adam Joshua started feeling a lot

better. A little sympathy from Ms. D. always seemed to go farther than a lot of sympathy from a lot of other people.

Unfortunately, a little sympathy was all Ms. D. ever expected you to need before she expected you to get back to business.

So she headed out the door to run an errand to the office.

Adam Joshua looked around the empty classroom and finally settled for going over to sit beside Mortimer Flugg.

"I'm Adam Joshua," he said. He wasn't sure if you were supposed to introduce yourself to a skeleton, but he thought it wouldn't hurt to be polite.

"I was sorry to hear about the lion," he said. "I know a lot about things getting eaten up."

Although he had a feeling a skeleton with teeth marks on him probably wasn't going to be any too sympathetic about chewed-up planets.

"I was sorry to hear about your project," Mortimer said in a wavering, spooky whisper.

Adam Joshua scooted backward in a hurry.

45

Actually, when he thought about it, a sympathetic skeleton wasn't what he was looking for at all.

"Being gnawed on isn't very pleasant," whispered Mortimer.

"I wouldn't think so," Adam Joshua said, scooting faster.

Mortimer giggled a very familiar giggle, and Angie's head popped around the edge of a pile of books stacked behind the skeleton.

"Nelson told us about your project at recess," she told Adam Joshua. "We all feel really bad about it."

"Even Mortimer," she whispered in a quivering creaky way.

Everyone started pouring in the door, and a lot of people went by to tell Adam Joshua how sorry they were to hear about his planets.

It made a difference to know that at least people cared.

But there was one person who wasn't feeling the least bit sorry. "Too bad, so sad," a sneering Elliot Banks whispered.

———

Math wasn't something that went well with

feeling sorry for yourself, so Adam Joshua tried to put everything else out of his mind while he worked the day's problems.

Except that somewhere in the middle of his addition he had an idea.

It was a really amazing, absolutely terrific, stunningly spectacular idea. It was really scary to think that Mr. D. had inspired it.

He started drawing on his work sheet, and the more he drew, the better it became and the more excited he got.

"It's really great!" he shouted, scaring everyone around him.

"I can't believe there are people who like math that much," Heidi grumbled as Adam Joshua hurried to the front of the room to show Ms. D.

————

It took a lot of help from his parents that night to get it all wired right.

"But I don't mind one bit," his father said as he handed Adam Joshua the screwdriver to tighten the last screw. "I've never seen such a great invention."

Adam Joshua totally agreed, but as a scientist he thought he'd better stay calm about it and check things out.

He tied one end of a piece of string around his bed leg, stretched the string across his bedroom door, and tied the other end to a switch on his invention.

Then he whistled for George.

George showed up at the bedroom door looking surprised. Given the trouble he'd gotten into over the planet thing, he didn't expect Adam Joshua to be whistling for a few days.

Amanda Jane showed up right behind him. She didn't bother looking surprised. She just looked like she couldn't wait to get into Adam Joshua's room so she could start getting into things.

"Shadmorecookies," she said, pushing George out of the way. George followed behind, looking more than a little suspicious.

Amanda Jane ran into the string, and the string flipped the switch, and suddenly an alarm started going off, and a big red light started blinking, and a tape recorder started so that over all the commotion, very clearly, came the sound of Adam Joshua's voice booming, "GET THE HECK OUT OF MY ROOM!!"

"Badbadbadbadbadbad!" Amanda Jane howled, running out the door. George ran howling right behind.

Adam Joshua grinned, satisfied. If there was ever an invention that was going to save the world, this was definitely it.

Chapter Five

Adam Joshua and Nelson had so much Science Fair stuff to cart to school the next morning, Adam Joshua's mother had to take them in the car. Amanda Jane sat in the front seat and glared back at them, but she didn't say a word.

Adam Joshua was delighted to learn his invention had such a long-lasting effect.

Nelson couldn't believe it.

"I mean," he whispered, "I'd give anything just to have Henry be quiet for that long."

"Flibbleblat!" Amanda Jane told him with a spit.

Ms. D. might have told the big guys they had to move over at the Science Fair, but she must have forgotten to tell them they had to like it.

They were all grousing and griping when Adam Joshua and Nelson passed by.

"Who let those little kids in here?" a sixth grader yelped, outraged.

"Ms. D. said if they wanted to be in the Science Fair, they could be in the Science Fair," a fifth grader told him.

That sixth grader must have been new to the school.

"Well, who does that Ms. D. think she is?" he groused, and everybody around him stopped what they were doing and looked a bit astonished.

"Ms. D.," the fifth grader said solemnly, and everybody else gave strong firm nods.

As far as Adam Joshua was concerned, his class was setting up the most exciting exhibits around.

"And the big kids will be really amazed,"

Nelson said, cheerfully getting ready.

"FISH AND ESP—INCREDIBLE BREAK-THROUGH!" Nelson's sign read. "ONE OF NATURE'S BEST-KEPT SECRETS."

He put up a lot of charts showing how many times his fish got the numbers on the experiment cards right.

"I decided not to mention my math homework though," Nelson told Adam Joshua. "It's not Julius's fault he can't add."

He put out a second sign: "THE DREAMS FISH HAVE."

He'd drawn pictures of Julius's dreams, and Adam Joshua wasn't the least bit surprised to see that most had cute girl fish swimming around in them.

But there was one drawing that looked downright terrifying.

"That's the inside of Henry's mouth," Nelson told him. "Julius keeps having nightmares about it."

There were a bunch of teeth in the picture, and a tongue, and some big red round things.

"Tonsils," said Nelson.

———

Adam Joshua started setting up his exhibit, and several people came over to watch.

"Adam Joshua," Angie said, "that's absolutely the best invention I've ever seen!"

Everybody else nodded, and they all looked absolutely impressed.

Adam Joshua didn't even try for modest. At this point, he thought he deserved all the praise he could get.

He put up his sign.

"THE REALLY BIG PEST ALERT—FOR REALLY BIG PESTS!!" he'd written.

And he'd added pictures of Amanda Jane and George to show exactly what kind of pests he meant.

———

Adam Joshua and Nelson weren't the only ones who'd done a lot for science.

Angie had built a terrific maze. It had twists and turns, a ramp and a wheel, and a big red "X" to show where Walton Nine had died trying.

Heidi put a cup beside the exhibit with a note on it.

"New Hamster Fund," it read.

Adam Joshua and Nelson looked at the maze and the "X," and sighed while they put a dime each into the cup.

"Thank you for caring," Angie said softly.

"Anything to keep her from trying fish," muttered Nelson.

———

Philip had finally settled for drawing the insides of bodies, and a lot of body parts close up. He'd also brought in a lot of labels, and he put up his sign.

"GET YOUR BODY LABELED. ANY PART FREE!"

"OK," Angie told him. "I want to know exactly where my heart is, but I don't want to hear any details about how it looks."

Philip studied a picture in his dad's book, wrote "HEART" on a label, and drew a little smiling valentine beside it.

"I had no idea it was so cute," Angie said, pleased.

———

Sidney's brother's socks were spectacular. Red-and-gold checked ones were growing green mold. Blue-yellow-and-aqua ones were

55

growing orange fungus. A polka-dot one was growing some really impressive spotted mushrooms. And one sock really was growing something purple that looked like it'd never been grown before.

All together, they looked like a rainbow that had run amok.

Everybody gathered around the sign that said, "MY BROTHER'S SOCKS," and applauded while Sidney took a bow.

And Adam Joshua decided that as soon as he was speaking to George again, they were going to have to have a long talk about socks.

Ralph took a good close look at his own.

"Science really makes you think," he told Adam Joshua.

———

Heidi's exhibit was full of an awful lot of dead brown plants.

"WHAT HAPPENS TO PLANTS WHEN YOU SING TO THEM!" her sign read, and she had a lot of photos to show green healthy plants before the singing, and the same plants midway through the experiment definitely looking droopy and depressed.

She had a green plant sitting there with a sign, "SINGING DEMONSTRATION."

Adam Joshua and Nelson stopped by for a demonstration.

"Even though they keep dying, I try to pick songs to encourage them," Heidi said, clearing her throat.

It seemed to Adam Joshua that the plant looked nervous already.

Heidi sang a song she'd written about green green growing things never giving up, and she sang all the verses and added an extra chorus.

She wasn't very far along before Adam Joshua began to feel brown and curled around the edges himself.

"Those plants never stood a chance," Nelson told Adam Joshua as soon as they could politely hurry away.

———

Mr. D. dressed Mortimer Flugg in a top hat and bow tie, and wrestled him down to the gym.

He put a sign beside Mortimer that read, "THE GREATEST SCIENCE FAIR ON

EARTH!" and wired Mortimer's hand to point the way.

"He looks very nice," Angie whispered to Mr. D.

"It makes him feel needed," Mr. D. whispered back.

"We could probably get a lion for him too," Sidney offered.

There was a slight rattling, and every one of them could have sworn that Mortimer's bones shook.

———

Elliot Banks came in late so he could make a loud, noisy, smug, smirking, Elliot-Banks-has-arrived-and-you'd-better-notice-it entrance into the gym with his solar system.

Even the grousing sixth grader stopped grousing.

"Hey," he said, "that little kid looks OK."

"He needs to get to know him better," Angie grumbled to Adam Joshua.

Elliot took a lot more than his share of an exhibit table, and he looked around at the rest of the projects and shook his head in pity.

Then he caught sight of Adam Joshua's invention.

He moved a little closer to get a better look.

Adam Joshua had made a special recording for Elliot. So now he tried to look innocent and look busy and pretend he didn't see Elliot sneaking up to flip the switch.

The alarm went off, the light flashed, and Adam Joshua's voice boomed out.

"BEAT IT, YOU INCREDIBLE JERK!"

Elliot turned a furious red, opened and closed his mouth a few times without saying a word, and stomped away.

"I just love science," Angie said, giggling.

Adam Joshua felt a warm scientific glow, himself.

As an inventor, he felt great knowing the Pest Alert got rid of several kinds of pests.

Chapter Six

Anybody who was worried about the future of the world would have felt a lot better at the Science Fair.

Kid scientists showed how to recycle, and how to save energy, and all the great stuff that can happen when you plant more trees.

Kid inventors showed off robots, and new ways to swat flies, and better ways to boil water.

The big kids really were amazed at all the exhibits Adam Joshua's class had brought.

"I mean, this stuff's terrific," the grousing sixth grader said.

Everyone was properly astonished about fish and ESP.

And a lot of people gained a lot more respect for their socks.

———

Adam Joshua's invention was a big hit.

"Because it's just terrific," Ms. D. told him.

In fact, everybody liked the Pest Alert so much, they started placing orders with Adam Joshua.

"I'd better bring you the stuff to make two," the grousing sixth grader said. "At my house we have twins."

"And I'll take the biggest, strongest one you can do," a fifth grader told him. "Like industrial strength. Just tell me what you need to make it, because you wouldn't believe my little brother."

"It's already industrial strength," Adam Joshua said. "You wouldn't believe Amanda Jane."

———

Mr. D. had decided to stay in case anybody needed help, but nobody did, and after a while he got bored.

A bored Mr. D. was a dangerous thing to have around.

First, he wanted to experiment with a fifth grader's volcano, but he added so much baking soda and vinegar, it erupted all over the place and ran in rivers down the aisles.

He moved on to a boomerang exhibit, and everybody ended up ducking like crazy, trying to protect their ears at the same time they were hopping around trying to keep their ankles dry.

He was just reaching an exhibit on earthquakes when a lot of people panicked and hurried off to tell Ms. D.

"But I love science," Mr. D. yelped as Ms. D. led him firmly away. "I plan to teach the baby everything I know about it."

"Before we save the world from everything else," Angie told Adam Joshua grimly, "we're going to have to save it from Mr. D."

———

After lunch it looked like business was

starting to get a little slow for Philip, so Adam Joshua took a break to go ask for a thyroid label.

"Terrific," Philip said, sounding relieved. "Either everybody asks for the same parts everybody else asks for, or else they ask for parts that are too gross to label."

Philip looked in his dad's book, wrote "THYROID" in big red letters, and put the label on Adam Joshua's throat.

Adam Joshua was very surprised. He hadn't known people had thyroids until lately, and he certainly hadn't known his was in such a public place.

They decided advertising might help, so Philip started making labels while Adam Joshua put them on Mortimer Flugg. He put "HEART" where the heart used to be, and he added in "BRAIN" and "LUNGS" and "APPENDIX."

Sidney stopped by to watch them for a few minutes.

"That lion must have gotten really full," he finally said.

Adam Joshua couldn't help noticing that a lot of people thought Elliot's solar system was pretty terrific until they found out Elliot didn't know the least thing interesting about it. Then they all looked terrifically bored.

"I can make it run at high speed and backward!" Elliot kept shouting after them as they walked away.

"That Elliot kid's really a jerk," the grousing sixth grader told several people.

"I knew he just needed to get to know him better," Angie said.

Finally Ms. D. went over and calmed Elliot down, and talked to him sternly, and made him go off with her somewhere.

When he came back, his arms were loaded down with books about planets, and he had a disgusted look on his face.

"Ms. D. told him he had to give her a really long and good report about the solar system next week," Angie said with a grin. "She also told him that if he had any questions, he should ask Adam Joshua."

Adam Joshua gave up on the being mad and not talking to George. This was just too great not to ESP home.

———

All day there had been a steady stream of people hotfooting it over to see Sidney's brother's socks.

Unfortunately, toward the end of the fair, Sidney's brother was one of them.

Everybody hurried to the rescue just as soon as they heard about it.

"CLOSED FOR REPAIRS," a sign on Sidney's exhibit said.

They found Sidney lying behind it tied and gagged with the most disgusting of the socks. Adam Joshua and Nelson untied and dusted him off while Angie went to get him a glass of water.

"Still worth it," Sidney said, spitting out some really ugly sock lint.

———

"Time to pack up," Ms. D. called out toward the end of the afternoon.

It was also time to pack Mortimer Flugg back to the classroom.

"Nope, no way, not me," Mr. D. said when they told him. "He bit me this morning, and I still have a bruise from where he kicked me the other day."

Adam Joshua and Angie carried the skeleton by his legs. Nelson and Heidi each took an arm, and Sidney helped out with the head.

"Don't take your eyes off him for a minute," Mr. D. warned them.

They all watched Mortimer suspiciously, and they moved slowly and carefully, and everything went fine until they were halfway along.

Suddenly there was a lot of commotion, and they all ended up in a heap heaped with everybody else. Most of Mortimer was heaped right in there with them.

"Except his head's missing," Heidi yelped after they'd gotten themselves sorted out.

"So's Sidney," Angie said.

It took a little while, but they finally found him lying in the middle of the floor down the hall.

Mortimer's teeth had a good tight bite on Sidney's nose.

"Don't even ask," croaked Sidney.

Ralph had been busy all day showing his collection of fingerprints and looking through his book so he could finger Mr. D.

Adam Joshua and Angie were just getting back to the gym when Ralph let out a shout and everybody came running.

"I'm not sure yet about Mr. D.," Ralph told them excitedly, "but Sidney's fingerprint exactly matches the fingerprint of Fat Lefty Malone!"

"But Sidney doesn't look anything like Fat Lefty," Angie said, as they all studied a picture in the *Book of Crooks*.

Fat Lefty had a lot of chins, and not much hair, and tiny mean eyes.

"Yep," said Mr. D., "that's him."

"But Sidney doesn't have a mustache," Angie told Ralph.

"Sidney's probably wearing a disguise," Ralph said. "And maybe he's shaved off his mustache. But fingerprints don't lie."

"If you were Fat Lefty and you wanted to wear a disguise," Philip said, "would you pick a disguise that made you look like Sidney?"

Sidney walked into the gym looking tired of socks, fed up with skeletons, and innocent of crime.

Ralph tackled and handcuffed him, made an official private eye's arrest, and got ready to drag him off to the police.

"But that's my nose print," Sidney kept yelling. "And I'm skinny, and right-handed, and I've never had a mustache in my life."

"That's what they all say," said Mr. D.

———

Half of Adam Joshua's class kept celebrating because they'd been so great as scientists, and the other half kept shouting out new ideas for next year's Science Fair. All together, it was hard to get any packing up done.

"I have a whole year to get a real body," Philip told them firmly. "And by the next fair, I'm going to have one."

"Don't tell Angie," Nelson whispered to Adam Joshua, "because I don't want her to help or get anywhere near my fish, but next year I'm going to try a maze in the aquarium."

"I'm not even showing up next year," Sidney hollered as Ralph dragged him along.

"Because you won't be out of jail yet," Ralph said, sounding stern.

Adam Joshua packed quietly. He had no idea what he was going to do for the fair next year, although something with George and ESP might be nice. It wouldn't go far toward saving the world, but George might be more helpful about science if he was part of it.

Still, the next science fair was a year away so he had a year to think it over.

Right now he had something more important to do.

Because this afternoon, just as soon as he could get home, he was going to shoo dogs and babies out of his room and set up his Pest Alert.

And then he was going to settle in and take his time to make this really incredible, super beautiful, absolutely terrific model of the entire solar system.

Right down to the tiniest glorious moon.